DOGNAPPED!

Jan Page

Illustrated by Nick Price

www.**booksattransworld**.co.uk/childrens

DOGNAPPED!
A CORGI PUPS BOOK : 0 552 546569

First publication in Great Britain

PRINTING HISTORY
Corgi Pups edition published 2000

5 7 9 10 8 6 4

Set in Bembo Schoolbook by
Phoenix Typesetting, Ilkley, West Yorkshire

Corgi Pups Books are published by Transworld Publishers,
61–63 Uxbridge Road, London W5 5SA,
a division of The Random House Group Ltd,
in Australia by Random House Australia (Pty) Ltd,
20 Alfred Street, Milsons Point, Sydney, NSW 2061, Australia,
in New Zealand by Random House New Zealand Ltd,
18 Poland Road, Glenfield, Auckland 10, New Zealand
and in South Africa by Random House Pty Ltd,
Endulini, 5a Jubilee Road, Parktown 2193, South Africa.

Made and printed in Great Britain by
Cox & Wyman Ltd, Reading, Berkshire

Contents

Series Reading Consultant: Prue Goodwin
Reading and Language Information Centre,
University of Reading

For David

Chapter One

The Witch and her Dog were
eating slugs on toast for
breakfast, when a gold envelope
arrived in the post. Inside was an
invitation.

"Ooh! How exciting!" said
the Witch. "I must buy a new
hat and get my nails sharpened."

On Friday afternoon the Witch
and the Dog arrived at Wizard
Wheeze's castle. He greeted
them at the gate.

"Welcome!" wheezed the
Wizard. "But where's your cat?
Didn't you bring her with you?"

"Oh, I don't have a cat any
more," replied the Witch. "I have
a dog." The Dog stepped
forward and held out his paw.

"Well, er, pleased to meet you, old chap," said the Wizard, surprised. "Tell me, can you do magic spells?"

"Yes," said the Dog. "I've just passed my Grade Four magic exam."

"With top marks!" added the Witch, proudly.

There was a loud hiss from
behind. Sooty, a large black
witch's cat, arched her back and
gave the Witch a nasty stare.

"I hate witches' dogs," she
snarled. "They shouldn't be
allowed!"

"Now then! We don't want any trouble!" wheezed the Wizard. "This is a party and you're all here to have fun. Park your broomsticks and come this way!"

A large cauldron bubbled away in the corner of the garden

and the Wizard served the
witches with glasses of stinging-
nettle wine. Mounds of food
were piled high on a table –
bat-burgers with beetle sauce,
fried spiders' legs, frog-fritters,
and green-slime trifle for
pudding.

"This is the best meal I've had
in ages!" cried the Witch, helping

herself to her fourth bat-burger.

When the witches had
finished eating it was time for
the party games. They played
Pin the Teeth on the Vampire and
had broomstick races up and
down the garden. Then it was
time for the Treasure Hunt.

Every year, Wizard Wheeze
buried a magic wand
somewhere in his garden and the
witch who found it could keep it
for herself. They weren't allowed
to use any spells to help them.
They had to sniff out the magic.

"Noses in the air!" shouted Wizard Wheeze. "Ready, steady, sniff!"

The witches got down on all fours and crawled round the Wizard's garden, sniffing as hard as they could.

"I'd love to win the wand," said the Witch. "Mine has nearly worn out, and I can't afford to buy a new one."

"Just leave it to me," replied
the Dog. He sat up and sniffed
the air. A faint smell of magic
was coming from the bottom of
the garden. "This way!" he
whispered.

The Witch and the Dog
tiptoed down the path, following
the smell as it grew stronger and
stronger.

"The magic wand is in there!" said the Dog, pointing to an enormous pile of garden rubbish. The Dog dived in and dug with all his might. Grass cuttings and potato peelings flew into the air and an old tea-bag landed on the Witch's nose.

"Hurry up!" called the Witch.
"The cats have spotted you,
they're coming this way!" The
other witches' cats arrived and
gathered round the compost
heap.

"Ugh! I'm not going in there!" said Sooty. "I've just had a bath."

"It's all slimy and revolting!" said a ginger tom called Charmer.

"And it smells disgusting," said a grey Siamese.

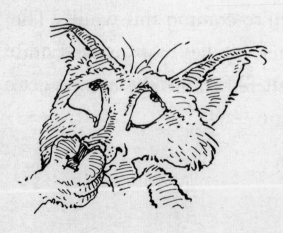

"Got it!" called the Dog, popping up with a beautiful magic wand between his teeth.

"Hooray!" cried the Witch. "We've won!"

"Well done, old chap!" said Wizard Wheeze. "I can see why the Witch wants a dog instead of a cat. Why, I think I might get a dog myself."

"Yes . . . cats are useless!"
muttered the witches, who were
all very bad losers.

"I'll never win anything with
a cat as my helper," said one
witch.

"I'm getting rid of Sooty,"
said another, whose name was
Cackle. "I'm going to buy myself
a dog!"

"Yes! That's what we need!"
cried all the witches together.
"Witches' dogs!"

Chapter Two

The next morning, the witches
threw out their cats and locked
the cat flaps. Then they flew
down to the local pet shop and
banged on the door with their
broomsticks.

"I want that black Labrador."

"An Alsatian for me!"

"Give me that poodle!"
shouted Cackle.

The pet-shop owner was delighted. Business had never been so good. He put a large sign in the window, saying, WITCHES' DOGS SOLD OUT.

Cackle took her poodle back to her bungalow and gave him a saucer of milk. "Come on, doggy, doggy," she cried.

The poodle growled and plonked himself down on the sofa. "Anything on the television?" he asked in a snooty voice.

"Not now!' said Cackle.
"Drink your milk and then you
can help me with my spells."

"Spells?" replied the poodle.
"You must be joking."

"I never make jokes," said
Cackle, firmly. "Catch me three
mice this instant!"

"Catch them yourself,"
muttered the poodle.

"I can't catch mice! I'm
scared of them. All witches are
scared of mice. Don't you know
that?"

"Don't know, and I don't care
either," sniffed the poodle. "I'm a
pedigree dog. I don't do jobs."

"Oh yes, you do! You're a witch's dog now and you've got to do as I say!"

"Witch's dog?" scoffed the poodle. "I've never heard such nonsense."

Suddenly there was a strange
sound coming from the garden.
Cackle rushed to the window
and looked out. Sooty and about
a dozen other witches' cats were
marching round the lawn,
caterwauling and hissing.

"Give us our jobs back!" they miaowed. "Dogs out, Cats in! Dogs out, Cats in!"

"Oh, bothersome broomsticks!" cried Cackle.

"They're squashing my deadly nightshade! . . . Quick! Quick!" she called to the poodle. "Chase those stupid cats away!"

"I'm not going out there,"
replied the poodle. "It's raining
and I've just had my hair done!"

"This is hopeless!" said
Cackle. She dragged the poodle
back to the pet shop and asked
for her money back.

"He's useless!" she told the
shopkeeper. "He doesn't drink
milk, he can't catch mice and
he's too big for the cat flap!"

The pet-shop owner scratched
his chin. "It sounds to me like
you need a cat," he said.

"A cat!" screamed Cackle. "A cat? Witches don't have cats any more."

"Then how about a hamster?"

"A witch's hamster!" snorted Cackle. "Don't be ridiculous! I want a dog like the Witch's Dog!" Then Cackle had a brainwave. "Of course!" she cried. "Why didn't I think of it before? I'll ask the Witch's Dog to come and work for me instead!" And she flew off to the Witch's house as fast as her broomstick would carry her.

Chapter Three

"What are you doing here?" asked the Witch, opening the door.

"Er . . . You invited me for tea," said Cackle.

"Did I?" The Witch was rather surprised. "I suppose you'd better come in then." The Witch trotted off to the kitchen to put the kettle on.

Seeing her moment, Cackle went up to the Dog and patted him on the back with her spiky fingers. "Come and work for me!" she whispered into his floppy ear. "You can live in my nice clean bungalow!"

"No thanks," replied the Dog.

"I'll buy you lots of juicy bones."

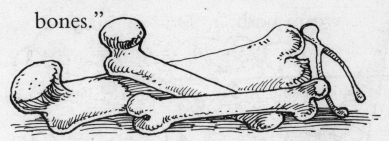

"I'd rather eat slugs," replied the Dog.

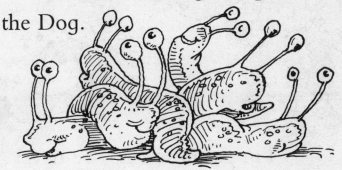

"I'll comb your fur and get rid of all your fleas."

"I like my fleas."

"Well, how about a lovely warm bath?"

"I'm proud to say I've never had a bath in my life," sniffed the Dog.

"Please be my witch's dog! I'll give you anything you want!" pleaded Cackle.

"No!" said the Dog firmly. "I will never leave the Witch."

"Huh," snorted Cackle. "We'll see about that." She picked up the Witch's new magic wand and waved it in the air.

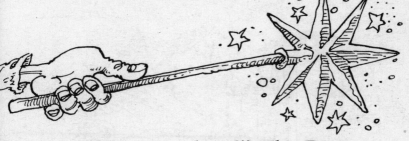

"Leave it alone!" The Dog pulled at her cloak. "It doesn't belong to you!"

"One-two-three, and off we go!

Take us to my bungalow!"

There was a puff of purple
smoke and Cackle and the
Dog disappeared!

"Tea's ready!" called the Witch. She tottered into the living room, with three mugs on a tray.

"How peculiar," said the Witch. She looked round the empty room. Something very odd had been going on. What was all this purple smoke? Why was her magic wand glowing? And, most important of all – where was the Dog?

Within a few seconds, the Dog found himself standing in Cackle's bungalow.

"Welcome to your new home, doggy!" said Cackle, rubbing her hands in delight.

"This is not my home and I am not your doggy," said the Dog, who was furious. "I'm leaving now."

"Oh, no, you're not!" cried Cackle, doing a quick spell. "I've just locked all the doors and windows. There's no way to escape!" She laughed wickedly.

"Now, let's do a spell to make all the witches fall off their broomsticks."

"I don't do those sort of spells," said the Dog.

"You do if you work for me!" chuckled Cackle. "Fetch me three mice — now!"

"No! I will never work for you. Take me back to the Witch!"

"Oh, bothersome broomsticks!" cried Cackle. "I won't feed you, or take you for walks. You can sit there and starve until you agree to be my witch's dog!" Cackle marched out of the room. Things were not working out the way she had planned!

Chapter Four

Three days passed and the Dog
was still a prisoner in Cackle's
bungalow. He felt so hungry!
Every morning, Cackle dangled
a fat juicy slug in front of his
nose and asked him if he was
going to help her with her spells.

He always said no, but time was running out. There was only one way that he was ever going to escape, and that was by magic! But he had no idea how to work Cackle's cauldron or where she kept her wand.

That afternoon Cackle flew off to do her weekly shop at the supermarket. The Dog watched her go and then searched the bungalow from top to bottom.

He looked in the wardrobes
and drawers. He looked under
Cackle's bed. He took everything
out of the cupboard under the
stairs, but he couldn't find
Cackle's wand anywhere.

Then he saw Sooty, sitting in
the garden, looking cold, hungry
and very sorry for herself. Of
course! Sooty would know
where Cackle kept her wand.
She would even know how to
work the cauldron. But would
Sooty help him? There was only
one way to find out.

The Dog ran into the kitchen and banged on the cat flap. Sooty glanced up and shot him a nasty look.

"Sooty!" shouted the Dog. "I need your help!"

"Forget it!" Sooty hissed back. "We've lost our jobs and it's all your fault."

"I'm sorry!" replied the Dog. "I didn't mean to do it. Cackle has dognapped me. If you help me escape, I will do everything I can to help you get your jobs back."

Sooty's ears pricked up at this. She padded over to the cat flap. "What have you in mind?"

"Cackle has made a spell to lock all the doors and windows. If you can tell me where her wand is, I should be able to undo the magic and get out."

52

"That's easy. She keeps her wand in the fridge."

"The fridge?" said the Dog, very surprised. "I would never have thought of looking in there!" He rushed to the fridge and sure enough, there was the wand, lying in a plastic sandwich-box.

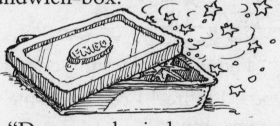

"Doors and windows, open
    wide!
Help this dog to get
    outside!"

The Dog waved the wand and said some extra magic words. In a flash, all the windows and doors sprang open! Sooty bounced through the cat flap.

"Thank you, Sooty!" cried the Dog. "I'm free! I can go home to the Witch!"

"Not so fast," said Sooty. "You promised to help us cats get our jobs back, remember?"

"Of course I did!" said the
Dog. "Now let's think . . . what
can cats do, that dogs can't?"

"Catch mice," said Sooty.
"Witches are terrified of mice,
but they need them for their
spells. That's why they have cats
– usually," she added.

"I've got it!" cried the Dog.
"Let's make a spell to put
hundreds of mice in all the
witches' houses! The dogs won't

be able to catch them and the witches will have to ask their cats to come back!"

"That's a great idea!" said Sooty. "But we'll have to hurry. Cackle will be back any moment."

Sooty switched on Cackle's cauldron and turned the dial to "Animal Magic". The Dog thought back to his Grade Four magic exam and remembered the perfect spell.

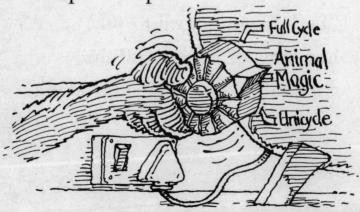

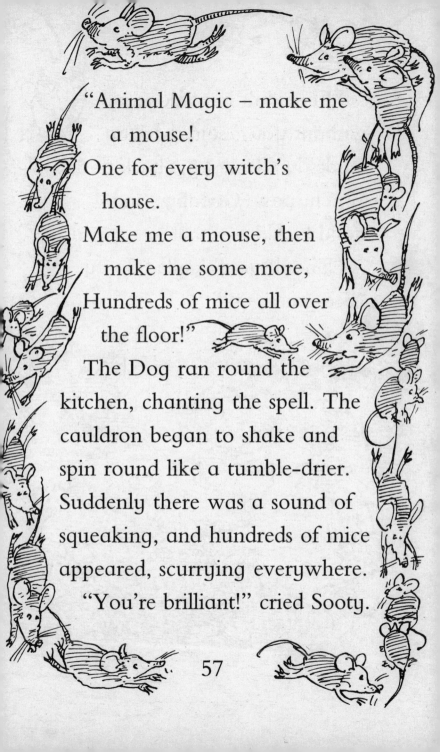

"Animal Magic – make me
a mouse!
One for every witch's
house.
Make me a mouse, then
make me some more,
Hundreds of mice all over
the floor!"
The Dog ran round the
kitchen, chanting the spell. The
cauldron began to shake and
spin round like a tumble-drier.
Suddenly there was a sound of
squeaking, and hundreds of mice
appeared, scurrying everywhere.
"You're brilliant!" cried Sooty.

57

"I couldn't have done it without you," said the Dog, modestly. "I must get back to the Witch, now. Goodbye and good luck!"

"Thank you!" called Sooty. "See you soon!"

There was a screech of brakes
outside as Cackle skidded to a
halt on her broomstick. Sooty
jumped through the cat flap and
hid behind a dustbin.

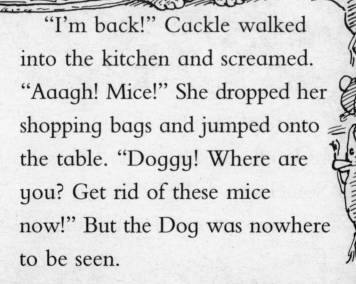

"I'm back!" Cackle walked
into the kitchen and screamed.
"Aaagh! Mice!" She dropped her
shopping bags and jumped onto
the table. "Doggy! Where are
you? Get rid of these mice
now!" But the Dog was nowhere
to be seen.

"Help! Help!" shouted Cackle as loudly as she could. "Please! Somebody, help!" Hearing her cue, Sooty leapt through the cat flap.

"Oh, Sooty! Am I glad to see you! Please get rid of these mice for me!"

"Only if you promise to give me my job back," said Sooty.

"Of course! Get rid of these mice and you can have anything you want!"

"Cream on my cornflakes? Fresh salmon every day for tea?"

"Yes, yes, anything!"

"Very well," said Sooty. She ran round the room and chased all the mice out of the house.

Cackle jumped off the table
and gave Sooty an enormous
kiss. "It's so good to have you
back," she said.

The Dog ran home as fast as he
could.

The Witch could hardly
believe her eyes. "You're back!"
she cried. "I was so worried!

Where on earth have you been?"

"Cackle dognapped me," said the Dog. "She kept me locked up in her bungalow. But with Sooty's help, I managed to escape."

"Sooty helped you?" gasped the Witch. "But I thought you were enemies!"

"Not any more," replied the Dog. "I did a spell to help the cats get their jobs back. Now Sooty and I are good friends."

"And I thought you'd left me!" said the Witch.

"I'll never leave you," the Dog replied, giving her a big soppy lick.

The Witch smiled a black toothy grin. "And I'm never, never, going to let you be dognapped again!"

THE END